Bad Luck, Lucy!

First published in 2007 by
Franklin Watts
338 Euston Road
London
NW1 3BH

Franklin Watts Australia
Level 17/207 Kent Street
Sydney
NSW 2000

A CIP catalogue record for this book is available
from the British Library.

ISBN 978 0 7496 7158 7 (hbk)
ISBN 978 0 7496 7302 4 (pbk)

Series Editor: Jackie Hamley
Editor: Melanie Palmer
Series Advisor: Dr Hilary Minns
Series Designer: Peter Scoulding

Printed in China

Franklin Watts is a division of
Hachette Children's Books.

Bad Luck, Lucy!

by Sue Graves

Illustrated by Lisa Williams

W

FRANKLIN WATTS
LONDON • SYDNEY

Sue Graves

"Have you ever
found something
that's lucky?
I haven't yet ...
but I keep
on looking!"

Lisa Williams

"Lucy reminds me
of how I used to be
when I was little –
I used to spread
paint everywhere!"

Lucy found a shiny coin.
"That's lucky!" said Dad.

She took it to show Mum.

But she fell over
the cat.

"Bad luck, Lucy," said Mum.

She took it to
show Gran.

13

But she spilt
Gran's drink.

15

"Bad luck, Lucy,"
said Gran.

She took it to
show Grandad.

But she knocked
over the pots.

"Bad luck, Lucy,"
said Grandad.

"This shiny coin is not lucky at all!" said Lucy.

Notes for adults

TADPOLES are structured to provide support for newly independent readers. The stories may also be used by adults for sharing with young children.

Starting to read alone can be daunting. **TADPOLES** help by providing visual support and repeating words and phrases. These books will both develop confidence and encourage reading and rereading for pleasure.

If you are reading this book with a child, here are a few suggestions:

1. Make reading fun! Choose a time to read when you and the child are relaxed and have time to share the story.

2. Talk about the story before you start reading. Look at the cover and the blurb. What might the story be about? Why might the child like it?

3. Encourage the child to reread the story, and to retell the story in their own words, using the illustrations to remind them what has happened.

4. Discuss the story and see if the child can relate it to their own experience, or perhaps compare it to another story they know.

5. Give praise! Remember that small mistakes need not always be corrected.

If you enjoyed this book, why not try another TADPOLES story?

Sammy's Secret
978 0 7496 6890 7

Stroppy Poppy
978 0 7496 6893 8

I'm Taller Than You!
978 0 7496 6894 5

Leo's New Pet
978 0 7496 6891 4

Mop Top
978 0 7946 6895 2

Charlie and the Castle
978 0 7496 6896 9

Over the Moon!
978 0 7496 6897 6

My Sister is a Witch!
978 0 7496 6898 3

Five Teddy Bears
978 0 7496 7292 8

Little Troll
978 0 7496 7293 5

The Sad Princess
978 0 7496 7294 2

Runny Honey
978 0 7496 7295 9

Dog Knows Best
978 0 7496 7297 3

Sam's Sunflower
978 0 7496 7298 0